For Enzo

First U.S. edition 2013

Library of Congress Catalog Card Number 2012950562
ISBN 978-0-7636-6607-1

13 14 15 16 17 18 FGF 10 9 8 7 6 5 4 3 2

Printed in Shenzhen, Guangdong, China

This book was typeset in Goudy Infant.
The illustrations were done in gouache.

Nosy Crow
An imprint of
Candlewick Press
99 Dover Street
Somerville, Massachusetts 02144

www.nosycrow.com
www.candlewick.com

Pip and Posy
The Snowy Day

Axel Scheffler

nosy crow

An imprint of Candlewick Press

It was a very snowy day.
Pip and Posy wanted
to go out and play.

So they
put on their
warm sweaters . . .

their striped socks . . .

their puffy coats . . .

their waterproof boots,
their cozy scarves,
and their woolen mittens.

Then they went out
into the snow.

Wherever they walked,
they left big footprints.

They caught snowflakes on
their tongues.

They even made snow angels with big wings.
They were having so much fun.

Then they pulled their sled
up to the top of the hill . . .

and zoomed down
the other side.

"WHEEE!"
they shouted.

Then Posy had an idea.
"Let's build a snowmouse!" she said.

"But I want to make a snow**rabbit!**" said Pip.

"Snow**mouse**,"
said Posy.

"Snow**RABBIT**," said Pip.

Posy was so mad at Pip that she threw
the snow creature's head at him.

Oh, dear!

Then Pip was even angrier with Posy,
so he pushed her very hard
and she fell in the snow.

Oh, dear!

Now Pip and Posy
were both **very** cold
and **very** sad.

Poor Pip! Poor Posy!

Then Posy did a very kind thing.

"I am sorry for making you
all snowy, Pip," she said.

"And I am sorry for pushing you,"
said Pip.

They decided to go back inside,
where it was nice and warm.

They took off all their wet things.

And then they got out their clay
and made mice *and* rabbits.

And frogs and pigs and birds, and elephants and cows and giraffes!

Hooray!